NINJAGO
Masters of Spinjitzu

Nothing in the Dark

D0492127

Contents

Friend or Foe?   4

Snake Power   6

Who Needs a Hug?   8

Spin in Style   16

Armed and Armoured   18

Nothing in the Dark   20

Amazing Snake Facts   36

The Last of His Kind   38

Ninja Quiz   40

Friend or Foe?

He had already been betrayed once, and Lloyd Garmadon was about to be let down again. My nephew – an aspiring evil-doer – planned to lead one snake tribe into battle against another, but ended up with both tribes turning against him. Now there were twice as many snakes for him to take his revenge on! Upon overhearing how greatly they fear 'the Anacondrai', Lloyd decided to open one more tomb...where he found Pythor, the last surviving member of this feared tribe. The two lonely souls immediately became friends – but the snake had fiendish plans of his own.

Snake Power

The Constrictai: a Serpentine species so strong that they can crush stone in their powerful coils. They waited many moons to see daylight again – but it was not Lloyd Garmadon who set them free. It was his new friend, Pythor. Pythor stole Lloyd's map of snake tombs and used it to release the strongest (if not the brightest) of all the Serpentine. His evil masterplan was coming together...

Who Needs a Hug?

Kai and Cole were getting ready to leave on a scouting mission when they heard an explosion. With their weapons drawn, they were ready for just about anything, from a snake attack to Lloyd Garmadon trying to steal more sweets.

What approached them, however, was not a fearsome villain or thieving kid. It was Jay, covered in ash from head to toe, his ninja robes scorched and blackened. He looked frustrated and disappointed.

"Oh, not again," said Cole, shaking his head.

"What was it this time, Jay?" asked Kai.

"Explosives," grumbled the Ninja of Lightning. "One touch, and boom!"

"That is illogical," said Zane, walking up to join the other three. "You would have been blown up!"

Jay's voice rose as he began to lose his temper. "It was an outwardly-directed explosion, Zane. And it would have worked, but I used a little too much dynamite... and I got the timer wrong... and I didn't notice that the wind had changed direction."

Cole looked at Kai. There was no need to say anything. Since the appearance of a new snake tribe the week before, Jay had been desperately trying to come up with a defence against an attack. The Constrictai were not as sneaky as the Hypnobrai or the Fangpyre, but they didn't need to be. They were so strong that if they wrapped their coils around you, they could easily squeeze you until you passed out.

Jay's idea was to try to develop ninja robes that the Constrictai wouldn't want to embrace. So far, he had tried a robe covered in broken glass, one that burst into flames if you touched it, one covered in slippery fish oil, and now one primed to explode. They had all been spectacular, and painful, failures.

"So what's next?" asked Kai, almost dreading the answer.

"I'm the Ninja of Lightning, right?" Jay answered. "So I run a few hundred thousand volts through the robes, and when the snakes attack, zap!"

Cole put a hand on Jay's shoulder. "And if your nunchucks, or anything else metal, brush against your robes, zap! I think we have to face the fact that defending ourselves against the Constrictai won't be that easy."

"Hmmmm," said Zane.

The other three ninja turned to look at their companion. They all knew what that kind of "hmmm" meant. Zane had an idea.

"It is insane," Zane warned them. "Dangerous too. But there's a one in a million chance it would work."

"It has to be better than Jay blowing himself up twice a day," said Kai. "Let's hear it."

* * *

Two days later, the ninja were ready. It had taken that long to convince Kai and Jay that this plan had any chance of working. Even Cole had been reluctant, insisting on mapping out multiple escape routes in case things went badly.

They had decided to test Zane's idea on a Constrictai patrol spotted by Kai a week earlier. There were only four snakes, so the ninja had a good chance of being able to fight their way free if they had to.

The Constrictai warriors were surprised to see four ninja waiting for them on the road. They were even more puzzled by the fact that none of the ninja were holding weapons.

"Ninja," said one of the snakes.

"We can ssssqueeze them," said another Constrictai. "They don't sssstand a chance."

The ninja started walking slowly toward the snakes, arms outstretched. "Come on, guys," said Kai. "They look like they could use a hug."

"Yeah," said Jay. "Let's give 'em a big old squeeze. That always makes the day brighter."

The Constrictai glanced nervously at each other, before backing away. "Ssssomething is wrong," said one of the snakes. "Why do they want to hug us?"

"It must be a trap," said another. "No one would choose to embrace a Constrictai warrior!"

"They must have a ssssecret weapon," said a third. "It will be triggered when they touch us."

The ninja kept walking, with big smiles on their faces and arms open wide as if they were greeting old friends. "What are you so worried about?" Cole asked the snakes. "Maybe we just decided we should all be friends."

"Sssssnakes are not friends with humans!" one of the Constrictai spat. "This is all a trick — a trap! But you will not fool us!"

"We will retreat," said another snake warrior, turning to slither rapidly away. "We will be back when we have discovered the ssssecret of your new weapon."

The ninja stood in the road and watched as the snakes fled. When they were long gone, Cole exhaled in relief. "Wow. I can't believe that worked."

"We did what they least expected," said Zane. "That led to confusion, and confusion led to fear."

"Amazing," said Jay. "We've got Spinjitzu, golden weapons, fighting skills – and we won this battle with smiles and hugs."

"It's a weird old world," said Kai, leading the group back toward camp. "And that's a fact."

Spin in Style

My ninja fight strong enemies, so need strong protection. They have mastered an ancient martial art, but deserve a modern look.

"Battle claws!"

"The material is really light and breathable."

"Whoa! Cool armour!"

"I love the gold highlights!"

Sensei Wu asks

It was no surprise to see the boys so happy with their new uniforms. Can you guess who said what about their clothes?

Armed and Armoured

Like all predators, snakes are well-equipped for hunting, as well as for protecting themselves against their foes . . .

1. Snakes have teeth of different kinds for different purposes. The long, scary, sharp fangs are used for injecting venom or catching prey. If a snake loses or breaks a fang, it will grow another.

2. Rows of rear-facing teeth in both jaws are used to keep prey from escaping. When prey is swallowed, the throat muscles push it into the stomach for digestion.

3. Snakes have lots of very strong muscles and their back bones are made up of 100-400 vertebrae! That is why they are so flexible.

4. The skin of a snake is a real suit of armour. Entirely covered in scales, it protects the snake against attack from other predators. Even the eyes are protected by transparent scales instead of eyelids!

5. Snakes do not chase their prey, but they can move very fast. Rough scales on their bellies allow them to keep their grip on different surfaces, such as tree bark or rocks, so they can ambush their prey.

6. Snake scales are made of keratin, just like human fingernails! They are almost completely waterproof, which means that snakes are able to hunt even in heavy rain.

Sensei Wu asks

Many snakes grow out of their skin and get rid of it several times a year, just like an old sock. True or false?

Answer: True. Snake scales are made up of layers of cells. The outer cells are dead and protect the living ones underneath them. When the snake sheds the dead skin, it rubs up against a rough surface to rip the outer layer, the snake sheds the dead skin. It rubs up against a rough surface to rip the skin and simply slides out of it.

Nothing in the Dark

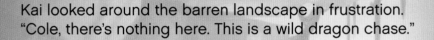

Kai looked around the barren landscape in frustration. "Cole, there's nothing here. This is a wild dragon chase."

Since this particular snake tribe rarely ventured above ground — preferring to use a network of tunnels — he was certain that there would be signs of their presence. The earth would be disturbed, for example, or there might be holes where they had emerged onto the surface. So far, though, there was nothing to see.

"Maybe your information was mistaken?" asked Zane.

Cole shook his head. "No. The snakes have been near here. I can smell them."

Zane raised an eyebrow. "Really? I wasn't aware the Constrictai had a particular smell. Plus, I've found them not to be clammy as people expect, but to be dry to the touch and –"

"Zane!" Kai snapped. "You're an encyclopedia of snake knowledge, we get it."

Cole crouched down, his eyes scanning the ground for any sign of snake activity. They had been searching the area for most of the day. It was a day that could have been spent gathering supplies, training, or doing other things to prepare for the inevitable fight with the Constrictai. Instead, here they were, at Cole's request, with nothing to show for their efforts.

It was Kai who made the discovery. "Hey, over here!" he cried. Cole and Zane rushed over to where he was standing. At first, Cole saw nothing.

The dirt was smooth as could be and there was no hole. But Kai wouldn't have called them over without a reason, so Cole took a closer look.

That was when he realized that the earth was too smooth and even. Someone had raked over it to hide any trace of a disturbance. Once Cole saw that, he found that he could spot other places where this had happened too. They formed a trail leading to the east. The three ninja followed it for about two hundred metres until they came to a pile of branches.

"What do you think?" Kai asked Cole.

"I think you already know the answer," Cole replied. He started pulling the twigs away, aided by Kai and Zane. When they were done, they had uncovered a hole.

"So they were here," said Zane. "We should report this to Sensei Wu."

Cole peered down into the darkness. "Not 'were'...I think they *are* here. Otherwise, why go to so much trouble to hide their tracks? Remember what the Sensei told us – Constrictai stay in dens underground, whenever they can. I think this is a den entrance."

"I was not aware Constrictai ever made any effort to disguise their presence in an area," said Zane. "They are, on the whole, arrogant and violent and fear nothing . . . not even other snakes. Why would they feel the need to conceal their lair?"

"I don't know," said Cole. "Could be there's something valuable in this den they didn't want the other snakes to find. Maybe a weapon, or secret plans, or even food stored for the winter. Who knows what snakes would consider to be important? There's only one way to find out, though."

"Let me guess," said Kai. "We're going down into the deep, dark hole after them."

"Right," said Cole. "We'll confirm they are hiding here and then tell the Sensei. He'll know how best to flush them out...or seal them in. Zane, you stay up here. If Kai and I aren't back in an hour, go and find the Sensei and Jay and tell them where we are."

Cole jumped down the hole, followed by Kai. It was pitch dark and musty at the bottom. "I can't see a thing," Cole said. "We'll have to risk using torches."

"Remember when you were a kid," Kai said, "and you always thought there were things hiding in the dark? Then you grow up and find out there's usually nothing there at all."

"If you're lucky, there isn't," said Cole.

As the pair of ninja ventured deeper into the tunnel, the light from their torches revealed a shadow moving about fifty metres ahead of them.

"We've got company," whispered Kai.

The two ninja moved quickly but cautiously down the tunnel. When they reached the spot where they had seen the shadow, they found that the tunnel split into two branches. "There could be a whole nest of Constrictai waiting for us down either route," Cole said.

"Or down both," said Kai. "But...maybe there's just one guard down here who could give us valuable information, if we can catch him. Let's take the chance."

Cole thought for a moment, and then nodded. "All right. We split up. But at the first sign of snakes, get out of here. Don't start a fight you can't win."

Kai laughed softly. "Boss, there is no fight I can't win."

* * *

As Kai moved off down the tunnel, he repeated in his head what he had just said to Cole. The Constrictai were some of the toughest foes the ninja had ever fought. All they had to do was wrap their coils around you, and you were finished. If you spotted them before they attacked, Spinjitzu would send them flying. If you didn't, well, you wouldn't have much time to feel sorry about it.

He reached out to feel the walls of the tunnel as he walked. Kai expected them to be solid rock, but instead, they were just packed soil. With no braces or beams, he wondered how the tunnels kept from collapsing. The idea of being buried down there sent a shiver down his spine and he quickened his pace.

Kai had just gone around a bend when his fear became reality. Loose dirt started cascading down from both sides. The walls were collapsing! He spotted the shadow moving far ahead, but didn't have time to worry about it. The dirt was already up to his knees and rising fast.

He began to whirl, hoping Spinjitzu could blow the soil away from him. As he turned into a whirlwind of fire, the effect was unexpected. The raw heat transformed the dirt into hard clay, stopping the landslide in its tracks. This tunnel, at least, wouldn't be coming down again any time soon.

Kai moved on, coming to what looked like a dining chamber. He had always wondered what Constrictai ate . . . but he had never expected what he was about to see.

* * *

Cole found his way blocked by booby traps, but not the kind one would expect from snakes. There were buckets of water propped over doorways, badly disguised holes dug in the floor, and even a fake skeleton who looked a little like one of the warriors the ninja had fought not so long ago. But Cole saw no sign of Constrictai.

He passed into a large chamber. There was a table in the centre and a little stool. Scattered on the table were pieces of old parchment, obviously worn from having been handled many times. He wondered if they were the snakes' secret plans. At least then there would be something valuable to take back to camp.

He glanced from side to side to make sure there were no snakes hiding in ambush. Once he was sure the way was clear, Cole slipped to the centre of the room and peered at the parchments. What he saw made his eyes widen in surprise.

* * *

Cole and Kai reached the exit at the same time, both talking over each other.

"The Constrictai eat ... sweets and pretzels?" said Kai.

"The snakes read old '*Adventures of Sensei Wu*' comics," said Cole.

"Wait a minute," the Ninja of Fire said. "Are you thinking what I'm thinking?"

"The Constrictai built this place, but they aren't living here," said Cole. "And now we both know who is."

"Help!" someone cried.

Both ninja rushed toward the sound. They knew the voice – it belonged to Lloyd Garmadon, the son of their greatest enemy. As they rounded a corner, they saw Lloyd caught in the coils of a Constrictai.

"This one invaded our home," snarled the snake. "He is ours to do with as we will."

"I didn't know they were still here, honest!" snivelled Lloyd. "I just thought it would be a cool place to hang out!"

Cole shrugged. "Go ahead," he said to the snake. "He means nothing to us. Let's go, Kai."

The two ninja turned and started walking away. The snake tightened its grip on Lloyd. Suddenly, Cole did a backflip from a standing start and planted both his feet in the startled Constrictai's face. The snake released its hold on Lloyd. Recovering, it lashed out with its tail, sending Cole flying. Kai charged, using a combination flying fox kick and panther strike to bring the snake down.

Kai helped Cole to his feet. There was no sign of Lloyd, who had run off during the battle.

"Okay, so what do we tell Sensei Wu about all this?" asked Kai.

"Simple," Cole answered. "Tell him this time there really was something in the dark."

Amazing Snake Facts

There are some things about snakes that scare even the bravest. But there are also some truly amazing facts that make even the most terrified want to learn more about snakes.

1. The biggest snake species in the world is found in the rain forests of Southeast Asia. It is the *reticulated python*, and it can grow up to ten metres long! That's the length of a small city bus!

2. The fastest snake in the world is the African *black mamba*. Apart from being one of the top ten most deadly snakes, it can move at a speed of twenty kilometres per hour!

3. The thickest known snake is the *anaconda*, which lives in tropical South America. The biggest one ever found measured thirty-five centimetres in diameter. It was huge – like a tree trunk!

4. The *anaconda* could also be described as the most peace-loving snake. It spends most of its life in the dark waters of the Amazon River where nobody can disurb it, and it is rarely seen on land.

5. The *Barbados threadsnake* is the smallest known snake species. It is only around ten centimetres long, and as thin as a toothpick.

6. The Australian *inland taipan* is regarded as the most venomous land snake in the world. It must be quite unhappy with its reputation, as it is very shy and always prefers to escape from trouble.

Sensei Wu asks

The king cobra *is considered to be the most intelligent of all known snakes. True or false?*

Answer: True. In captivity the king cobra can tell its handler apart from other people. Males in the wild tell apart and defend their territory, and females build nests out of leaves and twigs to lay eggs in. Such behaviour has not been observed in other species.

The Last of His Kind

Pythor P. Chumsworth was bored and lonely in his hidden lair. Of course, this was due to the fact that he had eaten his entire clan, so you could say he asked for it. Pythor was quite excited to befriend my evil brother's son and become his henchman. Just like Lloyd, that sly snake just loved eating ice cream, stealing sweets from kids and destroying things. Alas, the last of the Anacondrai also had far bigger plans: he wanted to become the leader of the united snake tribes and take over the whole world!

Ninja Quiz

No task is too difficult when you are well prepared. After reading the stories carefully, see if you can answer these questions.

1. What were Kai and Cole startled by in the first story?

2. What new invention was Jay testing out?

3. How did Zane describe his idea of fooling the Constrictai?

4. How many Constrictai were in the patrol the ninja met?

5. How did the snakes react to the ninja's "secret weapon"?

6. Who discovered the snakes' hideaway in the other story?

7. What did the ninja expect to find in the tunnel?

8. What did Kai do when the tunnel started collapsing?

9. Who was captured in the coils of the Constrictai?

10. What strategy did the ninja use against the snake?

Answer: 1. A sudden explosion, 2. Snake-repelling clothes, 3. Insane and dangerous, 4. Four, 5. They escaped as fast as possible, 6. Kai, 7. Weapons, secret plans or food for winter, 8. He used Spinjitzu to blow the soil away from him, 9. Lloyd Garmadon, 10. Bluff and attack.